Withdrawn

94

Big Trouble for Tricky Rabbit!

Other Books by Gretchen Will Mayo

Star Tales: North American Indian Stories About the Stars

Earthmaker's Tales: North American Indian Stories About Earth Happenings

Meet Tricky Coyote!

That Tricky Coyote!

Here Comes Tricky Rabbit!

Illustrated by Gretchen Will Mayo

Whale Brother

Native American Trickster Tales

Big Trouble for Tricky Rabbit!

Retold and Illustrated by
Gretchen Will Mayo

Walker and Company ✸ New York

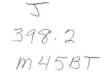
For Jean Crane and Barbara Joosse,
my sisters on a path.

First published in the United States of America in 1994
by Walker Publishing Company, Inc.

Published simultaneously in Canada by Thomas Allen and Sons Canada, Limited,
Markham, Ontario

Library of Congress Cataloging-in-Publication Data
Mayo, Gretchen.
Big trouble for tricky rabbit!/ retold and illustrated by Gretchen Will Mayo.
p. cm.
Includes bibliographical references.
ISBN 0-8027-8275-2. —ISBN 0-8027-8276-0 (lib. bdg.)
1. Indians of North America—Legends.   2. Rabbits—Folklore.
3. Trickster—Juvenile literature.   I. Title.
E98.F6M33 1994
398.2'08997—dc20   93-29749
CIP
AC

The art for *Big Trouble for Tricky Rabbit!* was painted with opaque acrylics on watercolor
board.

Book Design by Brandon Kruse

Printed in Hong Kong

2 4 6 8 10 9 7 5 3 1

Contents

Acknowledgments

Many people and institutions helped me generously when I researched the Rabbit stories and pictures. I send thanks and admiration to Dr. Jay Miller, D'Arcy McNickle Center for the History of the American Indian, the Newberry Library, Chicago; the Milwaukee Public Museum and its library staff (especially Judy Turner); the Kansas City Public Library; the University of Wisconsin system for use of its libraries; Joseph Bruchac, Abenaki storyteller and author; Amelia Cornelius, Oneida storyteller and author.

I am especially grateful to Margaret Jensen, whose understanding of young children and whose expertise in the early reader's process has contributed greatly to the crafting of this book.

Big Trouble for Tricky Rabbit!

Watch out!

Big trouble ahead for Tricky Rabbit.

Never fear.

He may be small,

but Rabbit says, "I can take care of

myself!"

Rabbit made the ocean to save himself

from Panther.

Once he shouted so loud that the earth

quaked.

What tricks will Rabbit try next?

Rabbit's Tail

Long ago, Rabbit had a long, bushy tail like other animals.

"I have the most beautiful tail in the world," Rabbit liked to say. But something happened.

Rabbit was feeling mighty happy one day. Snowflakes floated like feathers all around. Rabbit dashed through the flakes. He dashed around the willow tree. "Look at that!" cried Rabbit. "When I run, my tail is more beautiful than ever." Rabbit ran and sang:

> It snows! It snows!
> If only it keeps snowing,
> I will run and run and run.

Sure enough, the faster Rabbit ran, the faster the snow fell.

Rabbit, with his beautiful tail, ran all day long. The snow grew deeper and deeper.

Finally, day turned into night. Sleepy

Rabbit looked for a place to rest beneath a bush. But so many flakes had fallen, all the bushes were hiding under the snow.

Rabbit stood on the snow piled high. "How about that!" he said. "Now I am as tall as the willow tree." Then Rabbit laughed. "I am so tall that I can reach willow tree's green buds." Hungry Rabbit nibbled one. "Yum!" He nibbled another. "Yum, yum!" He ate until his middle was round. Then Rabbit lay down on a branch. He fell fast asleep in the willow tree.

Rabbit was so tired. He didn't wake up when Sun rose over the hill. He didn't wake up when Sun's hot rays melted the snow. He didn't wake up until all the snow was gone.

Then Rabbit's eyes opened wide. He looked down. "What's going on?" cried Rabbit. "Where are the flakes like feathers? Where is the deep, deep snow?"

Spring had come. On the ground, the tasty plants were green. But there was Rabbit, high in the willow tree.

4

"A rabbit should not be in a tree like a bird," cried Rabbit. "A rabbit should be on the ground."

The ground was far, far away. Rabbit leaned over to look. But he leaned too far. Rabbit slipped and fell out of the willow tree. He crashed headfirst to the ground.

When Rabbit landed on his front paws, they became short. When he landed on his head, his lip was split. But worst of all, when he fell through the tree, Rabbit's tail caught in the branches.

Rabbit looked up from the ground. "Oh,

no!" cried Rabbit. "I've lost my beautiful tail!" There was Rabbit's tail, high above. It hung from the top of the willow tree.

Poor Rabbit. He tried and tried, but he could not reach his beautiful tail.

Now Rabbit and all his grandchildren hop-hop-hop on short front legs. Now rabbits have split lips and short tails. Now the pussy willow grows lots and lots of little rabbit tails on her branches to tell us when spring is here. And rabbits never, never climb trees.

The Haudenosaunee (Iroquois) story of how Rabbit lost his tail, split his lip, and shortened his front legs is very old, and yet each storyteller has made it new. Jesse Cornplanter learned the story from his Seneca fathers when he was a little boy. He included it in a collection of stories from the Iroquois that he wrote in the 1930s.

Today the Abenaki poet and storyteller Joseph Bruchac weaves his own lively version of Rabbit's story. He warns that pussy willows are a reminder of what can happen if we are too proud, as Rabbit was about his tail.

Amelia Cornelius is a Wisconsin Oneida storyteller who graciously shared her story of Rabbit and the pussy willow. "Rabbit's Tail" is adapted from her version. Like Joseph Bruchac, Amelia Cornelius is careful to keep alive the spirit of this well-loved story while telling it as only she can, from the heart.

Stories change, but they also stay the same.

Rabbit's Tug-of-War

Thirsty Rabbit needed a drink of water. Bop!
Bop! He jumped over to the creek. But
someone else was there first. Tie-snake was
hiding in the water. Oh, no!

Rabbit zipped behind a tree. "If Tie-snake
sees me, he will grab me. He will carry me
away," thought Rabbit. "I will take a drink
somewhere else."

Rabbit ran over the hill. He found a new
spot on the creek. But Rabbit still was not
alone. There was fierce Man Eater. He was
thirsty too.

Rabbit jumped behind a tree. "I do not want to be Man Eater's lunch," said Rabbit. "I will wait until he leaves." Ho-hum.

While Rabbit waited he tap-tapped his foot. "Man Eater is a big bully. Tie-snake is too," he thought. "Two big bullies. One little rabbit." Rabbit tap-tapped his other foot. "But this little rabbit has a great big idea." He dashed into the woods.

Rabbit looked all around the woods. He found a long grapevine. Then he carried the vine back to Tie-snake.

9

"Tie-snake," called Rabbit. "You always talk big but you aren't very tall. I bet I am stronger than you are. I'll bet I can pull you out of the water."

Tie-snake looked up and said, "What are you up to now, crazy Rabbit? Everyone knows I am stronger than you."

Rabbit grinned. "Don't be too sure. I dare you to a tug-of-war. Grab the end of this grapevine."

Tie-snake stretched his long, thick body. "You don't stand a chance, Rabbit, but I will play your game."

"This is a long, long vine," said Rabbit. "Stay here while I run to grab the other end. When I call '*Pull*,' the contest will begin."

So Tie-snake waited.

10

Rabbit dashed over the hill. He carried the other end of the grapevine to Man Eater.

"Grrrrrrr!" growled Man Eater.

"Simmer down," said Rabbit. "You always talk big, Man Eater, but you don't scare me. I am strong."

"What a laugh," said Man Eater. "I could swallow you in one bite."

"Don't be so sure," said Rabbit. "I bet that I can beat you in a tug-of-war. Grab the end of this grapevine."

Man Eater said, "Rabbit, you are crazy." But he grabbed the vine.

"This is a long, long vine," said Rabbit. "Stay here while I run to grab the other end. When I call *'Pull,'* the contest will begin."

So Man Eater waited.

Rabbit dashed to the top of the hill. He saw

Tie-snake holding one end of the vine. He saw Man Eater holding the other end. He shouted, *"Pull!"*

Man Eater pulled and tugged and pulled one end of the vine.

Tie-snake tugged and pulled and tugged the other end.

"Wow! You are really strong!" Rabbit shouted from his hiding place. "I will have to pull harder."

Man Eater heard Rabbit. He pulled harder than ever.

Tie-snake heard Rabbit too. He pulled harder than ever.

Tug-pull. Tug-pull. What a lot of hard work!

"When did Rabbit grow so strong?" thought Tie-snake.

"How can Rabbit tug so hard?" thought Man Eater.

Rabbit wasn't tugging anything. He was sitting on the hill laughing.

Tie-snake and Man Eater tugged until they were worn out.

"I quit," said Tie-snake, and he crawled away.

"I quit," said Man Eater, and he crawled away.

Rabbit hopped down to the creek for a long drink of water.

Tie-snake is a fearsome character in South-eastern Indian stories. In some stories, Tie-snake carries off children and even adults to his den beneath the waters.

American Indian audiences know that Man Eater is a large cat, such as the mountain lion or cougar.

The Southeastern Creek, Natchez, and Hitchiti tell stories of Rabbit's tug-of-war with Tie-snake or other creatures. Watt Sam, a Natchez storyteller who lived near Braggs, Oklahoma, warned that these stories should be told only in cold weather or bad luck would follow. Recordings were made of many of Watt Sam's stories from the Natchez, Cherokee, and Creek nations in the early 1900s.

Rabbit in a Hurry

Rabbit dashed out of the woods. Zip! Rabbit raced right past Coyote.

Coyote stared at Rabbit's footprints in the snow. "Why is Rabbit in such a hurry?" thought Coyote. "Something must be chasing him. Something big. Something mean. It might get me too!" So Coyote dashed after Rabbit.

Zip! Coyote raced right past Wolf.

Wolf stared at the footprints in the snow. "First Rabbit ran past. Then came Coyote," thought Wolf. "Why are they in such a hurry?  Something must be chasing them. Something big. Something mean. It might get me too!" So Wolf dashed after Coyote and Rabbit.

Zip! Wolf raced right past Grizzly Bear.

Grizzly Bear stared at the footprints in the snow. "'First Rabbit ran past. Then came Coyote. Then came Wolf," thought Grizzly Bear. "Why are they in such a hurry? Something must be chasing them. Something big. Something mean. It might get me too!" So Grizzly Bear dashed away after Wolf, Coyote, and Rabbit.

Soon Grizzly Bear ran right up to Wolf, who was resting in the snow.

"Why did you run away from me?" asked Grizzly Bear.

Wolf answered, "I ran because Coyote ran."

"Then I will ask Coyote," said Grizzly Bear. He followed Coyote's footprints. Wolf came too.

"Coyote, why did you run away from me?" asked Grizzly Bear.

Coyote answered, "I ran because Rabbit ran."

"Then I will ask Rabbit," said Grizzly Bear. Coyote and Wolf came too. They found Rabbit resting in the snow.

"Rabbit, why did you run away from me?" asked Grizzly Bear.

"Yes, Rabbit, why the rush?" asked Wolf.

"Tell us, Rabbit. What's your hurry?" asked Coyote.

Rabbit answered, "I was eating in the woods. Wind came and blew snow down on

me. Then a branch fell from the tree. I was so scared, I jumped up and ran away."

Coyote, Wolf, and Grizzly Bear stared at Rabbit.

"What *big* thing chased you?" they cried together.

"Only *you* were chasing me," said Rabbit.

Grizzly Bear's fierce look melted into a grin. "What do you know!" said Grizzly Bear. "I fooled myself."

"What do you know!" said Coyote and Wolf. "We fooled ourselves."

Coyote, Wolf, and Grizzly Bear fell in the snow laughing.

Rabbit laughed too. "Hee, hee, hee."

"Rabbit in a Hurry" is adapted from a story told by a Kutenai named Pierre Andrew. He was thirty-three years old when Franz Boas recorded his stories and many others in the summer of 1914. The Kutenai have always lived in the area of the Rocky Mountains where Montana, Idaho, and British Columbia meet.

Rabbit Goes Fishing

Rabbit was out walking when Fox came along. What was Fox carrying? Rabbit walked closer to see. It was a string of fish. "What luck!" thought Rabbit. "Fox has lots and lots of fish. I am very, very hungry."

"Hey, Fox!" called Rabbit. "What a lot of fish you have. Do you have enough for me too?"

"No way," answered Fox. "I caught these fish all by myself. I am going to eat them all

by myself too. Go catch your own fish."

How rude.

Rabbit had never gone fishing. He didn't know how to catch a fish. But Rabbit didn't want to say that. So Rabbit was quiet as he followed Fox down the path.

Fox bragged and bragged about his fish. Rabbit listened. Ho-hum. But Rabbit was thinking too.

Soon Rabbit said, "So long, Fox. I have to go now."

"Where are you going?" Fox asked.

"To catch some fish of my own," said Rabbit. "Wish me luck."

"You'll need all the luck you can get." Fox laughed. "I've never met a rabbit who knew how to catch fish."

Rabbit hopped off the path into the thicket. He dashed through the thicket to pass Fox. When he was far ahead of Fox, Rabbit hopped back onto the path. Then he lay down. Rabbit lay very, very still. He looked just like a dead rabbit.

Soon Fox came along and saw him.

"How about that!" said Fox. "There is a dead rabbit right here on the path. I could have rabbit stew for dinner. But one rabbit isn't enough for a good stew. I have so many good fish." So Fox stepped over Rabbit and walked on.

As soon as Fox was gone, Rabbit jumped up. He hopped into the thicket. He dashed ahead of Fox. Then Rabbit hopped back onto the path and lay down again. He lay very, very still. He looked just like a dead rabbit.

Soon Fox came along the path and stopped

22

at Rabbit's feet. "What a surprise! Another rabbit is waiting to be my dinner!" cried Fox. "Two rabbits will make a good stew. But I have lots of good fish to eat." So Fox stepped over Rabbit and walked on.

When Fox was out of sight, Rabbit hopped back to the thicket, just like before. He ran ahead of Fox. He hopped onto the path and he lay down, just like before. Then, just like before, Fox came along with his string of fish.

"Wow! This is my lucky day!" cried Fox. "First I caught all these fish. Now I found all these rabbits. Three rabbits will make a super

stew. What a feast I will have!" Fox licked his lips. "But first I must get the other rabbits." So Fox put down his string of fish. He dashed down the path. He ran until he came to the spot where he last saw Rabbit. Where was he?

"Oh, no! Someone else must have grabbed my rabbit," cried Fox. "But so what! There is another one down the path."

Fox dashed down the path to find the other rabbit. He ran until he came to the spot where Rabbit played dead the first time. But Rabbit was not there.

"What's going on?" Fox frowned. "All the rabbits are gone." Fox's stomach growled. "Oh, so what! I still have lots and lots of fish to eat," said Fox. So Fox dashed back up the path. He ran past the spot where Rabbit had played dead. He ran right back to the spot where he had left his fish and Rabbit.

The fish were gone.

So was Rabbit.

"Oh, no!" cried Fox. "I've been tricked.

Rabbit has tricked me!"

Far, far off, deep in the thicket, Rabbit sat down for a feast. "Who says Rabbits don't know how to catch fish?" He laughed.

In 1927, Morgan Calhoun, a North Carolina Cherokee medicine man of sixty-four years of age, told the tale of Rabbit's fishing trip to a young Belgian anthropologist named Franz M. Olbrechts, who wrote it in a small notebook he carried with him. Calhoun had learned the story many years earlier from Tsi.sghwana.i, who was born in 1836. She likely had listened to her elders as they told the same story.

I Want My Teeth!

Rabbit was out walking when he passed Mountain Lion's house. Fierce Mountain Lion was gone. Good thing!

Rabbit felt brave. He marched right in. "Well, well, well," said Rabbit to himself. "Here I am all by myself in Mountain Lion's house. I think I'll look around."

He poked here. He snooped there. Then Rabbit stopped. "What's this?" he said. "It looks like Mountain Lion forgot something. Something important."

Sure enough. There were Mountain Lion's teeth lying on a log. Rabbit didn't waste a minute. He snatched Mountain Lion's teeth and ran away. Zip! He ran all the way to

Grandmother Rabbit's house.

"Look what I found, Grandmother Rabbit!" shouted Rabbit. He reached out and showed his grandmother Mountain Lion's teeth.

"Oh, my!" Grandmother Rabbit gasped. "Whose sharp teeth are those?"

"They're Mountain Lion's teeth. Now Mountain Lion can't eat us," said Rabbit. "I am a hero."

"Maybe," said Grandmother. "But Mountain Lion is fierce and strong. I have seen his sharp claws. He will be angry. He will come and get us."

Rabbit tap-tap-tapped his foot and thought. "You are right," he said. "Mountain Lion will surely come. But I think we can trick him."

Then Rabbit told his grandmother to build a fire. "Build it right outside the door," he said, "so Mountain Lion will see it when he comes."

Grandmother asked, "What will we do with the fire?"

"We will boil water in a big pot. Then I will put stones in the boiling water. When Mountain Lion comes, tell him we are making dinner for a guest."

"What guest?" asked Grandmother. "Where will you be, Rabbit?"

"I will be inside the house. I will pretend to be a guest who is talking to me. I will talk very loud."

"Sounds weird," said Grandmother.

"Trust me," said Rabbit.

So Grandmother and Rabbit went to work.

Soon Mountain Lion raced up to Grandmother Rabbit.

"Where is Rabbit?" he roared. "Where is that little troublemaker?"

"He's inside," said Grandmother. "Can't

you hear? He is talking to our guest."

Mountain Lion listened.

"Yackety-yackety-yackety-yack." Rabbit sounded like four people talking at once. "Yackety-yackety-yackety." What a lot of noise!

"So what," growled Mountain Lion. "I will tell that guest to get lost. Then I'll take care of that pesky Rabbit."

"Suit yourself," said Grandmother. She reached over and stirred the pot.

"Wait a minute," said Mountain Lion. "What are you cooking?"

"I'm making dinner for our guest," said Grandmother Rabbit.

Mountain Lion sniffed. "What is it? What's cooking in there?"

"Look for yourself," said Grandmother Rabbit. She scooped up some stones to show Mountain Lion.

"Rocks! You're cooking rocks for dinner?" roared Mountain Lion. "What kind of guest is here?"

"A big guest," smiled Grandmother. "A great big guest. The biggest guest you can think of."

"He eats rocks?" asked Mountain Lion.

"Of course," said Grandmother while she stirred. "Our guest loves to eat rocks. He says they are nice and crunchy. He says rocks will keep his big, shiny teeth sharp."

Mountain Lion backed away. "How long does your guest plan to stay here?" he asked.

"A long, long time," Grandmother Rabbit smiled again. "He is a good friend."

Then Mountain Lion turned and ran. He ran as fast as he could.

"Wait!" called Grandmother Rabbit. "Won't you stay for dinner?"

"No way!" cried Mountain Lion.

"Hee, hee, hee." Grandmother Rabbit laughed.

"Yackety-yackety-yack," said Rabbit inside.

"You can stop!" called Grandmother to Rabbit. "Mountain Lion doesn't want to look for his teeth after all."

"I Want My Teeth!" is adapted from a Caddo story told around 1904 by a man named Wing. Wing lived in Oklahoma, where many Caddoans live today. However, until they were forced to leave, early Caddoans made their homes in the area where Arkansas, Louisiana, and Texas meet.

Who Is Rabbit?

Rabbits are found throughout North America, from the cold arctic regions to the deserts. While their appearances vary as greatly as their environments, many characteristics are common to all. They are cute, with round eyes and soft fur, and they appear to be the most gentle, harmless of creatures. Given these features it is hard to believe that the trickster Rabbit created by American Indian storytellers could be so enduringly popular, until we remember that in life, as in the trickster tales, small and harmless does not mean incapable.

During the time of the trickster stories, every animal looked liked a human being, with head, hands, and legs. They were also subject to the same thoughts and emotions as human beings. It was only when they went outside that they put on the appearance of their species. As a character, Rabbit provided for an extended treatment of the innocuous. Through craft and trickery, he often got his way, as these stories attest. While others might misjudge him, he had the skill and confidence to best the big and humble the mighty.

Among tribes of the Great Lakes, as Manibozo or the Great Hare, Rabbit had aspects of divinity that enabled him to establish rules and traditions that people still observe. Most of the tales about Rabbit, though, focus on how he and other animals attained their looks and characteristics, and on the developing order of the world. As the stories unfolded and new stories were told, Rabbit split his lip, shortened his arms, and bent his legs. Many kinds of rabbits resulted. Most of the stories are about cottontails, but jackrabbits and arctic hares also came into their own by the time the world was finished.

The split lip so distinctive of rabbits received considerable attention in tales and everyday life. Parents were urged by their elders not to think about or look at rabbits so their baby would not be born with a harelip. Of course, some babies were born with this affliction and their parents were blamed for not paying attention to the needs of the unborn. As a result, the child got even more attention. Everything had its compensation, even disfigurement. Since American Indians lived in a world that was thoroughly interconnected, the actions of parents and of rabbits reflected on each other, but there were ways of dealing with the consequences.

The tribes of the East gave Rabbit much attention. While his flesh often appeared as dinner, his need to live was respected. People believed that rabbits would offer themselves willingly to be killed if prayers were made to explain that humans needed them for survival.

Western tribes treasured their rabbit-fur blankets during the cold winter months. Often, in Nevada and Utah, a blanket woven of strips of rabbit fur was the most valuable and useful thing a person owned. Children knew that they were adults when they were given fur blankets of their own.

In the cold North, Rabbit changed his coat with the seasons, turning white in winter. People were pleased that he was so helpful, giving them brown and white fur to decorate their clothing.

But rabbits had more to offer than themselves as food or their fur for warmth. Rabbits showed how to move through a tangle, living as they did in warrens, brambles, and undergrowth. They also lived in groups, which is how people should live. They got along with each other and raised large, happy families. They were gentle and herbivorous. Perhaps most important, their big ears show that they are careful listeners, and that may be the best lesson of all.

Jay Miller, Ph.D.,
D'Arcy McNickle Center for the History of the American Indian,
the Newberry Library, Chicago

Sources

The first people of the North American continent have a long tradition of storytelling. Often, however, their stories were recorded for the first time by non-Indians, usually scholars in the fields of anthropology and ethnology. We should always remember that these stories belong to the First People. We thank and honor those Native American Indians who shared their stories for the following reporters and publications:

Boas, Franz. "Kutenai Tales." *59th Bulletin of the U.S. Bureau of American Ethnology.* Washington, D.C.: 1918.

Bruchac, Joseph. *Iroquois Stories: Heroes, Heroines, Monsters, and Magic.* Freedom, Calif.: The Crossing Press, 1985.

Carpenter, Jesse. *Legends of the Longhouse.* New York: Ira J. Friedman, 1963. Reprint from *Empire State Historical Publication,* vol. 24. New York, 1938.

Dorsey, George A. "Traditions of the Caddo." *41st Publication of the Carnegie Institute.* Washington, D.C.: 1905.

Mooney, James. "Myths of the Cherokee." *19th Annual Report of the U.S. Bureau of American Ethnology.* Washington, D.C.: 1897-98.

Swanton, John R. "Animal Stories from the Indians of the Muskhogean Stock." *Journal of American Folklore* 26:194.

———"Myths and Tales of Southeastern Indians." *88th Bulletin of the U.S. Bureau of American Ethnology.* Washington, D.C.: 1929.

The following resources were consulted for background:

Current-Garcia, Eugene, ed. *Shem, Ham and Japeth: The Papers of W.O. Tuggle.* Athens: University of Georgia Press, 1973.

Dorsey, J. Owen. "Nanebozhu in Siouan Mythology." *Journal of American Folklore* 5:293-97.

Kilpatrick, Jack Frederick, and Kilpatrick, Anna Gritts. *Friends of Thunder: Folktales of the Oklahoma Cherokee.* Dallas: Southern Methodist University Press, 1964.

Lankford, George E., ed. *Native American Legends. Southeastern Legends: Tales from the Natchez, Caddo, Biloxi, Chickasaw, and Other Nations.* Little Rock: August House, 1987.